CORNERS OF MY MIND

BOOK 1: Memory is a fiction we keep rewriting

F. C. Holmes

Copyright © 2025 F.C. Holmes

All rights reserved

The characters and events portrayed in this book are fictitious. Any similarity to real persons, living or dead, is coincidental and not intended by the author.

No part of this book may be reproduced, or stored in a retrieval system, or transmitted in any form or by any means, electronic, mechanical, photocopying, recording, or otherwise, without express written permission of the publisher.

BOOK 1

Memory is a fiction we keep rewriting...

Dedicated to Colleen

"For sale: baby shoes, never worn"

Often attributed to Hemingway.

The English language is so powerful that, with just six words, it captures an entire lifetime of heartbreak.

INTRODUCTION

I've always been fascinated by how an entire universe can fit into a tiny handful of words. It's like a magic trick: you take a sliver of text—sometimes only a sentence or two—and somehow it resonates as deeply as a sprawling novel. In this book, we're diving into that very magic, the art of flash fiction and its even briefer cousins. But before we begin, let me walk you through the many shapes these ultra-short (and sometimes not-so-short) stories can take, because the literary world loves its labels. Each label comes with its own history, word count and charm.

I'll start with the smallest of them all—or at least the smallest I've encountered: the six-word story. You might have heard the famous example, "For sale: baby shoes, never worn." It's long been attributed to Ernest Hemingway, though most evidence suggests the anecdote is apocryphal, meaning it's more rumor than verified fact. Still, it's a haunting piece that shows how six words can spark entire chapters in our minds. It has led countless writers to try their own hand at telling stories in just six words.

Slightly roomier but still in the same minuscule realm is "hint fiction," a term credited to Robert Swartwood, who proposed that a story of 25 words or fewer—one that suggests a much larger world—qualifies as hint fiction. Think of it as a mere whisper on the page, where readers can't help but lean in to hear the rest. He coined the term in 2009, wanting to carve a niche for these pieces as presenting unresolved plots and characters that leave much to the imagination.

"Dribble" and "drabble" come next, each with an exact word limit. A dribble is 50-words, while a drabble is 100-words. The drabble has a colorful history: it's often said to have originated from the classic Monte Python sketch "All-England Summarize Proust Competition." Contestants in the sketch attempt to condense Proust's seven-volume novel *In Search of Lost Time* into a few seconds. This, in turn, is said to have inspired some modern-day writing challenges and is connected to people writing a novel in 100-words. Monty Python used the term *Drabble* in reference to a game involving quite novel writing. The name stuck and evolved. These days, drabbles flourish in everything from flash fiction anthologies to online writing challenges. The precise word count is part of the fun. Dribble is a half-sized, playful off-shout of the drabble.

Once we venture just a little bigger, we enter the territory of "microfiction," a broader label usually attached to stories up to 100 or 300 words, depending on whom you ask. The exact boundary is debatable, but microfiction has been around for quite a while—"micro" is simply a nod to the brevity. Some people also talk about "nanofiction," an even more whimsical term encompassing stories of 50 words or fewer. In either case, these extremely short works aim to capture a lot of meaning in very little space, often leaving the reader with a single striking image or a powerful twist.

Then there's "sudden fiction" and "flash fiction." These terms are sometimes used interchangeably, though "sudden fiction" typically hovers around 750 words and "flash fiction" is often pinned at 1,000 words or fewer. You'll see occasional references to 1,500 words for sudden fiction—boundaries in this realm are never carved in stone.

The idea of "flash" is that it's quick, immediate and impactful, like a camera flash illuminating a single moment in a character's life. In the late 1980s and early 1990s, editors Robert Shapard and James Thomas popularized "sudden fiction" by publishing anthologies of American short-short stories. Their work demonstrated the literary range and depth of short pieces, showing short fiction could truly be an art form with impact and reader engagement. Around the same time, "flash fiction" gained traction in various literary circles and magazines.

Moving on from these tiny tales, we hit the "short story," which is generally where mainstream literary tradition begins. There's no single, official rule, but a short story often lands somewhere between about 1,000 and 7,500 words. Most literary journals and awards recognize a piece in this range (or sometimes up to 10,000 words) as a short story.

If you stretch beyond that limit—say 7,500 to 17,500 words—you've got a "novelette." The word "novelette" can feel a bit quaint, but it's still used, especially in science fiction and fantasy awards, where the Science Fiction and Fantasy Writers Association (SFWA) has categories for these word counts. The SFWA categories are reflected in this introduction.

Longer than that is the "novella," usually occupying the territory from 17,500 words up to about 40,000. Over the years, the novella has played host to some of the most celebrated classics, from John Steinbeck's *Of Mice and Men* to George Orwell's *Animal Farm*. It's a form that offers more depth than a short story without demanding the commitment of a full-scale novel.

Finally, we get to the novel itself, the big fish in the literary ocean, generally starting around 40,000 words —though most modern novels clock in at 80,000 words or more. Epic fantasies and sprawling historical sagas often blast right past the 100,000-word mark, but once we're in "novel territory," the exact number is less important. What matters is that it's a sustained narrative that lets an author fully immerse us in another world.

These terms do overlap and publishers or critics do not

necessarily agree on the exact word counts. Still, I love how each term acts as a signpost on the path from single-sentence art to multi-volume masterpiece. In the collection within this book, we mostly live in the domain of flash fiction and below, where the thrill is capturing something immediate and electric in just a few paragraphs, sentences, or words. It's a challenge for any writer, but the rewards are enormous: what's more satisfying than giving readers an entire story in one breath?

I hope this overview helps you navigate the vocabulary and the word-count thresholds. As you read the pages ahead, remember that no matter what anyone calls it—dribble, drabble, micro, nano—each piece is written for one objective: ignite your imagination in the smallest space possible. And that, in my opinion, is one of the greatest feats good-writing achieves.

PREFACE

There is always some level of research involved in writing stories and verifying facts. For the most part, these narratives draw on my personal experiences and therefore require minimal research. When deeper investigation is necessary, I primarily rely on online sources, although libraries and periodicals also prove valuable. Inspiration, meanwhile, comes from everywhere.

As with most writers, these stories came from my presence on the planet. Some are about specific experiences, and some are collateral thoughts triggered by those experiences. Others just popped into my head. Where it makes sense, I give you some background on each story in an Author's note. Not all stories have one, nor do they need one. I will admit that well over one hundred souls—and many an unfortunate creature—are lost in these stories. The stories originate from the corners of my mind. My mind is a vast place; some corners are darker than others. I hope you will see that, just as life experience drives our thoughts, our passions, and our ability to express ourselves, I loved preparing this collection.

THE UNDERSTUDY

After decades of theatrical auditions, Miko is finally being recognized for his work. A letter from the Director of *The Play* arrives in the mail. Miko had auditioned for the lead role. *I don't want to read this alone,* he thinks. He throws on his coat and hat and runs to his brother Georgio's restaurant.

"Welcome, Miko!" exclaims the hostess. "Come, sit."

"Can Georgio see me right away?"

"I'll get him, Miko."

Georgio hurries over. "Miko, what is it?"

"I have a letter from the theatre."

"What does it say?"

"I haven't read it yet. I want you to read it to me, brother. I can't take another rejection."

"Yes, yes, I will."

Miko hands Georgio the letter. With great excitement, Georgio reads it aloud: "It is with great pleasure we offer you the position of understudy…" He stops reading. "What? They can't—"

"It's okay, Georgio. I get to study all the parts. If something happens to the lead actor, I get to take over. Things can happen."

"But Miko, you want the lead so badly."

"Yes, Georgio, but I'll still get paid. Maybe the next one."

Miko accepts the understudy offer. He learns his parts and proves himself to be better than the lead actor in many ways. The director takes a fancy to Miko, giving him more practice time than an understudy would normally receive.

Before the show opens, Georgio hosts a dinner for the cast and crew at his restaurant. Shellfish is not on the menu, since the lead actor, Keith, is allergic. Miko warns Georgio that the cast and crew enjoy drugs. Everyone shows up for the meal. Drinks flow freely. Conversation is lively.

The lead actress says to Miko, "You do so well as an understudy. Sometimes I wish you had the lead part instead of Keith. You're a better actor." She offers him some angel dust. "Put it in your drink. It'll add flavor—it'll be fun."

"No thanks," says Miko politely. He joins Keith, with the director and other cast members at a table.

"Anyone want some meth?" asks one of the actresses.

"Drugs make me sick," replies Keith.

The actress whispers to Miko, "Take some. It works like magic. No one will know."

Miko shakes his head no.

Uncomfortable, Keith moves to the bar. An actress joins him. Throughout the evening, several cast members admit they'd prefer Miko in the lead. Miko is repeatedly offered street drugs but consistently declines. It seems every cast member has a favorite drug. The night goes on, with drugs, food and alcohol all in abundance. Eventually, the party winds down. The next day is a rest day for everyone.

Before opening night, at the final dress rehearsal, Keith fails to show. One of the actresses suggests he may be sick after the party. The understudy, Miko, steps in to play the lead.

A detective arrives at the theatre, asking about the dinner at Georgio's restaurant. "What were people drinking?" he asks. "Were there drugs at the party? Was Keith's behavior unusual?"

"What is this about?" asks the director.

"Keith was found in an alley, slumped by a dumpster, with a rash on his face. He was taken to the hospital."

"Is he alright?"

"The hospital pumped his stomach. They found five different drugs and shellfish oil." Keith was allergic to shellfish.

On the night of the dinner, in the alley by the dumpster, Keith's leading role in *The Play* ends. A new actor takes over the lead: the understudy.

NIGHTMARE SQUARED

My mind goes blank. I fell asleep. There was nothing I could do. A stream of thoughts attacks me as before. I am pulled into my usual nightmare. The smell of fear is pervasive. I have been here before —a nightmare that repeats. I cannot move. Paralyzed. I recognize only the smell of fear.

I lie on a bed, exposed. Compressed against the sheets. Curtains from a nearby window peel away. They rise above me, form a fist and pound my chest. It is the same as always in this dream—this nightmare. But now, something is different. Something new.

The curtains wrap around my body. A darkness sets in. I am thrown through the bed. My paralysis is gone. My feet move. My hands are free. I'm falling. A nightmare's nightmare. The ground quickly appears, my face poised to hit. I gasp and awaken.

It's dark. It smells of fear. I lie on a bed, compressed against the sheets. The curtains are still. I dare not move. The stream of thoughts is dry. My mind is quiet. My body tries to stir. The sheets catch my legs. I cannot move. I try to relax. The darkness dissipates. Curtains from the window rise above me, form a fist and smash my chest. My head jerks forward. My eyes pop open. I gasp for breath. With sweat on my brow and a racing heart, I am now truly awake.

Author's note: Nightmare Squared

I have experienced both of these nightmares on separate occasions. Here, I combine them—one inside the other. I believe many people share a nightmare about falling; you just don't want to hit the ground.

CLICKETY CLACK

You step into the room—and the sound hits you first. Metal grinding against metal, shrill and scraping.

Then, the floor shifts.

You stumble, your balance gone in an instant. You crash down hard. The door behind you slams shut before you can turn back. There's no handle. Just the hiss of locking mechanisms sealing you in.

You rise. The ground trembles beneath your feet—not solid. Not still. A low, repetitive *clackety, clackety, clack* pulses through the space. The rhythm of a railcar in motion.

Thin beams of light slice through hairline cracks in the slatted wood wall. Dust dances in the shafts. You press your face to the wall and peer out with one eye. You see little—just the passage of trees and sky.

No windows. No roof hatch. No other exit.

It's just you, a prison, and a train engine.

The *clackety-clack* slows. A groan of brakes. The train shudders to a halt.

With a hiss and a sigh, the side door slides open.

You freeze.

Outside: nothing but sky.

Below: a river, churning a hundred feet down.

The rails stretch across a trestle bridge, frayed by rust and time.

And still—no one. Not a soul.

Then you hear it: the thunder of rotors.

A helicopter screams into view, blades slicing the air, edging closer. Figures inside. Faces shadowed. Rifles drawn.

Muzzles flash.

You don't think.

You jump.

Air claws at you. The wind howls past your face as the sky flips and spins. The river leaps upward to meet you.

Then—

Impact.

Icy cold. Bone-deep.

Your breath ripped away as darkness swallows the light.

No sound as you tumble down the river.

No pain as you fade into a deep, cold stillness.

PARKING LOT

The red car glistens in the sun. Rain runs across its hood. A special polymer shields the paint, an unblemished surface. After several days, the vehicle has not been moved. A warning ticket flaps in the wind under its wiper blades. A second ticket appears days later. A week passes.

A white plastic bin, a folded cardboard box and an orange pail rest in the bottom of a shopping cart that now sits beside the car. The cart arrived at the hands of the car's latest occupant, who opens the rear passenger door and climbs in.

The man has been seen in the area pushing a similar cart—this one blue with a large suitcase, a plastic bin, a cardboard box, an orange pail, blankets, a coat and a black garbage bag. At night, he returns to the car and climbs in. The shopping cart sits there until morning. The man disappears into the darkness of the car, only to reappear in the morning, his shopping cart full. During the day he wanders the streets.

Every night, the shopping cart takes its position by the car in the parking lot. Every morning, it makes the rounds. No one pays attention. Soon a silver cart appears beside the blue cart outside the car—this one empty. The next day, the blue-cart man is seen walking the streets with a second man pushing an empty silver cart. They work together toward a higher purpose.

That night, silver cart, the blue cart and a third person enter the parking lot. The carts are parked beside the car with the tickets in the parking lot. All three people disappear. The next day, the two men leave the parking lot with their carts. That night, they return with three more people. Five people enter the parking lot and vanish. The next day, the two men leave again, pushing their carts.

Business at the local bottle depot steadily declines. Regular customers are missing. The depot calls the police. A local detective comes to investigate. People notice that the blue- and silver-carted men travel every day to the parking lot, taking others with them. The others never return.

The detective goes undercover. He meets the men with the carts and travels with them to the parking lot. The detective touches the blue cart. They enter the parking lot. In the corner sits the ticketed red station wagon. They reach the car. The silver-carted man opens the passenger door. The detective is invited to stay the night. He climbs in. They follow. The detective falls asleep.

The next day, he wakes and fumbles his way out of the car. His shoes and clothes are different. He's taller. His hair is dirty, his face unshaven. Instinctively, he grabs the blue cart and strides toward the exit of the parking lot. The silver-carted man walks at his side. Tonight, it's his turn. The undercover detective is absorbed into the business.

The two now work together toward a higher purpose.

Author's note: Parking Lot

The mystery lies in uncovering what truly happened—a transformation? An absorption? Something beyond human comprehension. Definitely not of this world.

KIDNAPPED

It was a warm fall day when Mary enjoyed a margarita on her terrace. A car drove by—for the third time. She noticed because the driver looked like William.

Johnny, her husband and William his business partner, owned seventy-five trucks that hauled gravel for construction jobs all over the state. Even though Johnny was in business with William, Mary didn't much like William.

The phone rang inside the house. Mary went to answer it.

"Hello… hello?"

No one was there. She hung up.

Suddenly, all light vanished—a bag covered her head.

She screamed.

Strong arms wrapped tightly around her. She struggled. Her feet lifted off the ground. Mary kicked.

"Be quiet, lady or I'll kill you," a gruff voice said. Not a voice she recognized.

Mary stopped squirming.

"You cooperate and you won't get hurt," man said.

"Okay," Mary replied.

He set her down. She stood still as he tied her hands behind her back, then tightened the bag's drawstring around her neck.

They left the house.

"Climb in the car."

His hand guided her head so she wouldn't hit the car's roof. She stepped in and settled into the seat behind the driver.

As they drove, she memorized the turns.

The car stopped.

"Get out."

She stepped out. Into a building. Downstairs.

The air smelled of coal, cheap cologne, women's perfume and gunpowder. The scents were familiar. Could it be…?

"I want money from your husband and that bum of a partner of his," the man said.

"They probably don't want me back," she said.

"What do you mean?"

"Most of the work they do is for the mob."

"Who says they work for the mob?"

"Everyone knows. The mob has construction locked up throughout the state."

"Why wouldn't your husband want you back?"

"William's a hitman for the mob. Johnny runs the trucks. Johnny has women all over the state—he keeps me around for show. He won't pay for me. He doesn't care. But the mob? They don't like their secrets getting out. And I know secrets. I know William's secrets. When they find out someone knows William's secrets, they'll knock him off—clean as a whistle."

"I don't want nothing to do with the mob," the man muttered.

"It may be too late, sugar. You kidnapped the wife of a contractor who works for them."

Loud noises erupted upstairs, followed by multiple people stomping down a wooden staircase.

"William, what are you doing here? And why is Mary tied up?" Johnny asked.

"She says she knows my secrets, Johnny. She knows I'm a hitman for the mob. She couldn't possibly know that unless—"

Shots rang out.

Mary screamed.

Johnny yanked the hood off Mary's head and untied her hands.

William had dropped to the floor.

Three men stood behind Johnny, each armed, mafia-style. One of them had shot William between the eyes.

Johnny nodded to the men. They removed the body, cleaned up the scene, and left.

"You alright, sweetheart?" Johnny asked.

"Yeah. Thanks, Johnny."

They climbed the stairs.

They were home.

Mary poured herself another margarita. They sat on the veranda.

"I knew we went in a circle and came back to the house," Mary said.

"That was the plan, honey," Johnny said.

"Yeah."

"You did a good job, sweetheart. With William out of the way, the business is ours."

"I know, Johnny… and they'll never find out you talk in your sleep."

Author's note: Kidnapped

Hearing about a recent local kidnapping got me thinking. I imagined Johnny and William plotting together to kidnap Mary for ransom. But in a twist, Johnny and Mary would secretly conspire to kill William—both for financial gain and to remove him from their lives

THE MATHEMATICIAN

Jacob was at the top of his class in 1939. He graduated with honors from McGill University with a Science Degree in Mathematics. He and his friends often gathered at a local coffee shop and, over a cup of java, they tried to solve the toughest math problems known to man. It wasn't long before the Canadian Military recruited him for a special assignment—one for which he was aptly suited.

Jacob underwent intensive training in message decryption and spy detection. He was assigned to work on saving the lives of Canadian, U.S. and British forces during World War II.

Working in a high security bunker, Jacob's task was to decipher messages provided by allied forces that contained the location of enemy troops. He used four old codebooks. The books were in disarray, requiring extensive manual analysis. Soon, he noticed a troubling pattern: messages were consistently revealing allied troop locations rather than enemy positions. No enemy targets being identified. Speculation arose that the messaging system had been compromised. Jacob questioned why allied locations were on the messages instead of the enemy—but he said nothing. He suspected he was being watched.

One Tuesday morning, Jacob arrived at the bunker. A new officer was present accompanied by military police and high-ranking commanders. Of the twenty personnel that worked at the bunker, only Jacob deciphered messages. Two of the three communication specialists were escorted out of the bunker, along with five other personnel. Then, the codebooks on Jacob's desk were confiscated.

"Jacob, I am Colonel Charles Conroy. I am now in charge of this facility. You will say nothing of what happened here today. You will speak to no one about this. Leave the bunker and return in three days to your duties. Do you understand?"

"Yes, sir!" Jacob responded.

Jacob was escorted out of the code room. As he passed a steel door, he saw one of his colleagues in handcuffs being taken out of the bunker. Soon, Jacob found himself in an interview room.

"Put your hands above your head," an MP ordered.

Jacob complied. He was searched. The room was stark—just a steel chair, a table, a second door and a mirror. Jacob sat. He waited. What seemed like thirty minutes later, the second door opened. A man stood in the hallway.

"You know, Jacob, there's a spy among you," the man in the hallway said. "We will find the spy."

Jacob said nothing, then realized it was Colonel Conroy speaking to him.

"You're free to go. Be sure to return in three days. We need you."

Jacob was afraid and unsure what to do. Outside the bunker it was dark. He noticed a black car, its front seat illuminated by the red glow of two lit cigarettes. Were they there to watch him?

Fear gripped him. Perhaps they believed he was the spy? He had no family, no close friends. If they suspected him, was he a walking dead man?

Jacob went home and packed a bag, preparing to run, but he hesitated. He called his longtime friend Betty, a military officer.

"Betty, I'm scared."

"Are you at home?" she asked.

"Yes."

"Don't talk on the phone. Meet me where we first met. You remember?"

"Yeah."

"10:00 pm. Tonight."

"Okay," Jacob said. He waited at home until 9:00 pm. Through the window Jacob saw the black car —its dark silhouette the cat in a game of cat and mouse. Two red dots glowed in the front seat, like eyes that peered into the darkness, like a cat ready to pounce on Jacob's next move. He slipped out the back door and walked the two kilometers to the meet Betty. He ordered a scotch on the rocks and waited. Betty never showed.

Had they bugged his phone? There were two men watching from a table in the corner. Jacob got up to leave. When he stepped outside, the men grabbed him.

"Remember to show up in three days, Jacob," one of them said.

"Don't talk to anyone," the other warned.

Then, as if nothing had happened, they released him and walked away. Their black car sped off into the night. Terrified, Jacob stood there on the edge of the sidewalk. A Buick passed close by, its passenger-side mirror grazing him. Behind the wheel was Betty. In the passenger seat sat Colonel Conroy.

The car stopped beside him.

"Get in," Conroy ordered.

Betty was as pale as a ghost.

"I told you not to talk to anyone. I'm glad to see you haven't," Conroy continued. "You need to keep it that way, Jacob."

"Yes, sir!" Jacob replied.

"Betty, take us to Jacob's place."

As she drove, Conroy turned to Jacob. "You are very important to us. You must come back in three days. We have men posted here for your protection. If the spy had his way, you'd be dead by now. You're the only one who can work the coded messages. Let us do our job. Do you understand?"

"Yes, sir!"

"You have nothing to fear if you let us protect you."

Jacob remained in his apartment. On the third day, he stepped outside and the men in the black car greeted him.

"Come with us. We'll take you in."

Never before had he needed such protection. Why now? At the bunker, Jacob returned to his desk. The four codebooks had been replaced by one. The first message came in. He deciphered it. The book was perfectly organized. The first message revealed an enemy location. They had finally come to their senses.

No longer was Jacob deciphering allied positions. Under Colonel Conroy's command, strike success on enemy locations soared. Jacob deciphered the same number of messages as before, but now they were all enemy locations. The course of the war began to shift.

Colonel Conroy intensified his hunt for the spy in the bunker. Rumors swirled—he was closing in. Meanwhile, enemy losses continued to rise. Despite their setbacks, enemy forces had infiltrated the British Isles. Security at the bunker tightened. Then, a new kind of message arrived. Jacob decoded it. The message triggered his specialized training—training designed to expose spies. He delivered the message directly to a communication specialist.

"Code Mathematician," Jacob said.

The specialist transmitted the message.

The next day, "Did you hear the news?" one of the specialists asked Jacob.

"What news?" Jacob inquired.

"A house in Canada was bombed last night. Colonel Conroy was killed."

Author's note: The Mathematician

I woke up one morning after having a dream about a man in the military who was deciphering messages. He had an array of codebooks and, for some reason, was deciphering the positions of three different allied forces to determine a target location where those forces were not present.

There was no enemy in the dream. These locations made no sense to him. While he was at work, a figure of authority entered, confiscated all the decoding books and ordered him to leave. Fearing for his life, he complied.

His superiors observed that he has a more effective cypher method than the 3 books they provided. They consolidated his approach —but failed to inform him. When he left the bunker he was terrified and events spiraled out of control. In my dream, tensions escalated to the point of no return. When I put pen to paper, the story evolved further. Dreams are often muddled and have no clear ending.

In the story Colonel Conroy got too close to revealing the spy.

PARACHUTE

His parachute stayed in service until its collapse. The reserve was absent.

THE RESORT

The resort alarm blares, but what does it mean? People scatter, seeking cover—to no avail. Black-clad figures, masked and armed, storm through the grounds, rounding up guests. Their destination: the conference room.

Soon, twenty-five guests and ten gunmen gather there. Duffle bags litter the floor.

"Each of you, put on a jumpsuit," a gunman commands.

The captives obey. They climb into the jumpsuits. Now, everyone is dressed the same.

"You will be given a fake weapon and a blindfold. You must put on the blindfold and hold the weapon."

Now, there is no way to distinguish the gunmen from the captives. Seven captives separate from the group. Moments later, a bus pulls up outside. The gunmen and the seven board the vehicle, leaving behind a speaker in the conference room. A voice crackles from the speaker:

"No one move."

The bus speeds away.

"When the police arrive, they will assume all of you are gunmen. You will only be safe if you do what we tell you. Hold onto your weapons and remove your blindfolds. When the police arrive, do as they say. Only drop your weapons when they tell you, not before. We will be watching."

The police arrive. "Do as the police say," the voice on the speaker instructs.

Through a megaphone, an officer orders, "Put your weapons down and your hands on your head."

The captives comply. They are all arrested for conspiracy to kidnap. Each one faces interrogation.

"What have you done with the others?"

"We had nothing to do with this."

"The seven missing people are very wealthy. What did you do with them? We know you're involved."

"We're not involved. We are captives! They force us to put on jumpsuits and masks. They blindfold us and give us fake weapons."

The interrogator smirks.

"Yes, the matching jumpsuits, the speaker and your blindfolds were a clever touch." He leans in. "But your weapons? They're real."

THE ENVELOPE

Samantha receives a letter from her cousin—one she never expected. Anna, doesn't like Samantha. Anna never communicates with her and certainly never writes to her. Yet, here it is.

Samantha opens the envelope. Inside, Anna asks for ten thousand dollars to put toward a down payment on a car. Samantha dismisses the request as ridiculous but, to her own surprise, soon finds herself writing a check. She mails it to her cousin along with an insincere invitation: *Come by and take me for coffee in your new car.*

Two days later, Anna shows up at Samantha's door.

"I'm here to take you for coffee in my new car," says Anna.

"Wow. I'm surprised," replies Samantha.

"I am shocked that you sent me the money."

"Me too."

"Let's go," says Anna.

They go for coffee but don't have much to talk about. The truth is, they don't like each other. Samantha sips her coffee, increasingly perplexed by the situation. When Anna drops her off at home, Samantha sits down and writes to her again.

This time, she asks Anna to take her out for coffee again—but on the way, to stop at a gas station and steal a chocolate bar.

Two days later, Anna arrives.

"I'm here to take you for coffee in my new car. Here's your chocolate bar," she says, handing it over.

"Let's skip the coffee today, Anna. You can go home."

As soon as Anna leaves, Samantha writes another letter. This time, she instructs Anna to destroy all the letters she had received, then come by for coffee again. On the way, she must stop at a bank, rob it and bring back all the money. *Be sure not to get caught,* Samantha writes, *and bring this letter with you.*

Two days later, Anna shows up.

"I'm here to take you for coffee in my new car and here's the money from the bank," says Anna. She hands Samantha $127,000 in cash —and the letter Samantha had written.

"You can go home, Anna," says Samantha.

Samantha burns the letter in the fireplace and thinks about what she will have Anna do next. She wants to test her theory about the letters.

Samantha writes to her brother, asking him to deliver a banana, a stuffed monkey and a paper airplane inside a metal lunchbox.

Two days later, her brother arrives with the requested items.

Now she knows. Letters carry commands and their recipients must obey.

Samantha writes another letter to Anna, asking her to come and see her tomorrow. She knows Anna will receive the letter in one day and, as always, will arrive in two.

But Anna doesn't.

The letter sits on Anna's nightstand. Every morning, she reads it.

Samantha doesn't see Anna again.

THE CIRCUS

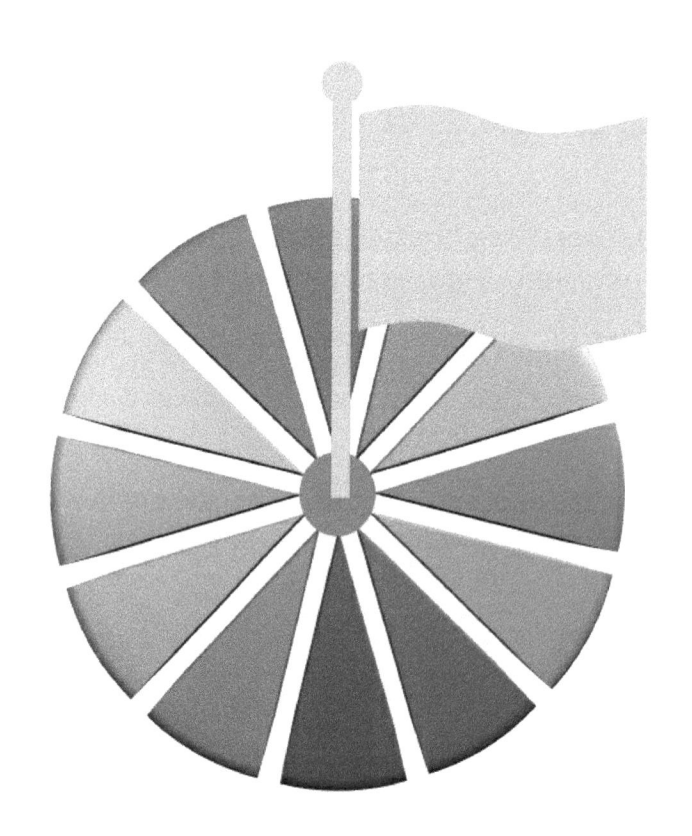

The ice fractures and breaks as Mike steadies himself, his rope taut. Tom's chill body stiffens, his fingers tighten around the belay. A distant echo rises from the depths as ice shatters on the rocks below. Mike stands on a fifteen-thousand-year-old ice plug that, according to satellite imagery, has recently melted enough to reveal a fourteen-hundred-foot deep cavern below.

Mike can't see past the lip of the ice. He takes a step. The surface trembles; his crampons hold fast. Suddenly, his feet drop from under him as the ice gives way—Mike goes with it. Tom grips the belay rope. Mike swings into the wall of the cavern and crashes hard. He's now fifty feet down and inside the cavern.

"Mike?" yells Tom

Mike is pummeled by shards of ice—tiny but numerous. He's under an ice overhang; more ice is ready to fall. Suspended in midair, now ten feet from the cavern wall, he calls back, "I'm okay. I'll take some pictures, get samples, then climb the rope."

The overhead sun perfectly illuminates the cavern. Mike lifts his camera. This is what he's here for: ice in the air, a crystal rainbow, solar reflections, shimmers of blue and green. The camera lens picks up a fluorescent glow. An aroma of mushrooms and strawberries drifts past Mikes nostrils as a green dust rises from the cavern floor, stirred by the cascading ice. Mike swings to the wall, scraping specimens into small jars. His task is finished. He ascends the rope, using ice axes to scale the thick ice and rejoins Tom.

"We did it, Tom. After being sealed for fifteen thousand years, we're here for its unveiling!"

"No kidding—this is epic!"

"Let's head home," says Mike.

They pack up their gear, having waited weeks for this moment. Soon, they're on the way back to civilization from the remote reaches of northern British Columbia.

Six months later, an inexplicable affliction spreads worldwide: women begin growing facial hair.

The medical community is baffled. Funds are raised. Research commences to find a cure. Some believe the disease originated in the cavern Mike and Tom explored.

Seven months later, a well-funded expedition returns to the site, led by Mike. Deep within the cavern, they discover the remains of two woolly mammoths that fell to their deaths twenty thousand years ago. Samples collected from the mammoths help researchers develop a cure for the hair-growth disease in women around the globe.

Mike and Tom are grateful to their expedition sponsors, a group whose livelihood was devastated by the outbreak: the circus performers known as the bearded ladies.

Author's note: The Circus

Picture that a cavern in northern British Columbia, sealed with ice for 15,000 years, that has been discovered. If a woolly mammoth is found within, it could be the source of a mysterious disease.

Also imagine a "what if" scenario and called it Hairdemic—a global condition in which women suddenly grow hair on their bodies. This unusual disease created an economic crisis for the bearded ladies at the circus, who ultimately solved the problem.

I combine the cavern narrative with the "what if" scenario to create this short piece of fiction.

The traditional Bearded Lady act at the circus has become increasingly rare. They were sideshow acts in the 19th and 20th centuries. Today there is sensitivity to exhibits that highlight physical anomalies in people. This is just a story, not meant to raise sensitivities.

THE TREE

More than 100 million years before the dinosaurs, a tree society existed. Prolific in ancient times, it grew increasingly rare as *Homo sapiens* dominance spread. That dominance is now waning. Humanity is diminishing. The Earth has been ravaged. The environment is threatened. *Homo sapiens* are an endangered species.

In a near role reversal, as life on Earth now courts extinction, the tree society gains strength. It begins to re-root. A society once diminished, re-emerges. The tree society offers refuge for humans —shelter from the elements, a place for mankind to thrive. Mankind's rebirth.

The ancient trees form a prehistoric society—a botanical order that sustains creatures who live in harmony with them. The tree society is hierarchical. The highest-valued trees are rare, coveted, powerful. They provide riches to those who care for them. These high-value trees shape, fashion and lead the society. Each level of the society enriches the levels below. Some trees and their leaves are rarer—more valued—than others.

Enrichment is achieved through consuming the trees and their leaves, which can be done in many ways. Mankind thrives in this environment, though he has yet to perceive the tree society. As humanity recovers from the brink of extinction, people begin to specialize. They learn to consume the forest. Humans become leaf-eaters. They build homes and harvest leaves. The tree society understands human consumption. Soon, humans learn to use the most common leaves—those at the bottom of the hierarchy—as currency.

As trade grows among humans, so does the struggle for power. They begin to recognize different trees and their rarity. A currency system develops based on that rarity, exposing the tree society's hierarchy to humanity. The rarest trees are difficult to find. Human trade soon reflects the forest's hierarchy. High-value trees hold greater worth for trade. The harmony between humans and the tree society tilts out of balance.

When humans discover these high-value trees, they claim them, guard them and harvest their leaves. The most ancient trees are uncovered and stripped. The harmony of the forest is broken.

The prehistoric society of trees—mankind's rescuer—becomes nothing more than currency for humans. A confrontation breaks out in the forest—a battle among humans, a struggle for power, a fight for resources. The most ancient tree commands the others to enact a change. Suddenly, every leaf on every tree transforms into the most common leaf. The tree society's hierarchy is no longer visible to humankind. Human currency is gone. The battle ceases. The power of the tree society is asserted.

Author's note: The Tree

This story began with a simple observation: a city worker blowing leaves off a sidewalk. That sight sparked the idea of a society in which humans live off leaves. I began to imagine what that might look like. While researching a mountain story, I learned the mountains dated back 2.2 billion years. This led me to wonder when the first trees populated the Earth—approximately 400 million years ago. That discovery inspired me to center this tale around an ancient tree.

A MURDER OF CROWS

The new nest on the edge of the Stenkin yard holds five baby crows. Five years later, the crow family has grown to over four hundred. Every year, they grow louder and messier. George Stenkin has had enough.

Mom and Dad, cousins, relatives and more baby crows—they all prosper on the edge of the Stenkin property. George loads his shotgun. He vows to cut the noise and the mess. Crows can recognize people's faces. Their offspring inherit that ability. The collective crow memory will be etched with George's face as he guns down the black birds. George's face will never be forgotten.

The crows return each year, nesting deeper in the woods. They keep their distance from George. He keeps his distance from them. Ten years pass.

No clouds in the sky. A sunny afternoon. George collects firewood, arms full. An unexpected solar eclipse appears—a pleasant surprise, perhaps. George looks up. The sky darkens. The trees darken. The woods go silent. It's not the season for crows to nest. George drops his wood and covers his ears, deafened by a chorus of "craw, craw, craw." A weight falls upon him—the weight of a murder of crows.

Author's note: A Murder of Crows

I watched a documentary about how crows pass on knowledge through their DNA to future generations. They can recognize people's faces. Their offspring inherit that ability. This allows the crows to inherently avoid dangerous individuals. After watching the documentary, I was compelled to write a story about this amazing ability.

I also watched the television series *Longmire*, where one of the characters pointed out to the sheriff that a group of crows is called a murder. That fact made it clear to me how the story had to end.

BOXCAR

The boxcar sits vacant for months in the rail yard. George now calls it home. The boxcar door slams shut. A forward lurch—metal grinds on metal. The boxcar comes alive.

George is inside, asleep. The smell of dust, hay and wood charges the muggy air. Dirt and hay shards alight on George's face. He awakens. Unmistakable railway sounds: rumbles and rattles, clangs and bangs, jerky movements. Stops and starts, back and forth. An engine collects cars to amass a larger train. George's boxcar home now sits in the middle of a larger, longer trainload of purpose. The train goes silent. All is still.

George hears a voice outside: "We're an engineer short today. One of our veterans didn't show. We'll finish our build of this train tomorrow."

George realizes he has one more night in his glorious boxcar. He opens the west boxcar door and peers into the sunset. The sun, atop a chain of motionless boxcars, descends. Pink, orange and yellow clouds blanket the sky. The sunlight pushes the boxcars against their shadows in an effort to light the rail yard. The boxcars clench the earth, blocking the sun's rays and casting long shadows toward George. A trainload of purpose, a distant fireball, exaggerated shadows, a planet in circular motion—this transition to twilight cannot be interrupted. The sun sets. The night sets in. George is home. He closes the west door and opens the east. Tomorrow's sunrise waits in silence. George falls asleep.

Dawn arrives. The sun streams in. George climbs out of the boxcar with his backpack and suitcase in hand. He secures both doors of the boxcar, crosses a few tracks and finds his new boxcar home. He tosses his suitcase onto the wooden floor. The smell of dust, hay and wood charges the air.

George walks back to his old boxcar train. He angles toward the engine. At the engine ladder, he stops, contemplating his next move. Then he ascends the ladder. The cab door is open. He peers inside.

"Well, look who it is! We missed your veteran ways yesterday, George. I hope you feel better," says the engineer.

Author's note: Boxcar

When I worked downtown I would buy newspapers written, published and sold by street people. They were entrepreneurs trying to scratch out a living, not asking for handouts. I would read the stories. Many of the stories were about the street people. Some of them were professionals who fell on hard times and ended up on the street. I felt compelled to write a story about a professional who fell on hard times and lived where he worked. Boxcar is the result.

THE CRAFT

Alarms blare as the crew runs to their escape pods. We jettison from the ship as it lists. My pod just clears the bulkhead. The ship cleaves apart. The Craft continue to fire at the pods as we descend.

Sparks threaten to ignite a fireball—an explosion gone wrong. There is no oxygen to burn in space. The pod protects me and the oxygen feeds my lungs keeping death at bay. Where am I? Where am I headed? The Craft continue to attack us. This hostile force fires first.

Our ship, disintegrates into pieces. My pod, captured by gravity, hurtles toward what I cannot see—a planet, I hope.

The heat is unbearable. My skin burns. My testicles want to explode. My lungs fail me. As quickly as the heat comes, it fades away. I can breathe. The pod cools. Gravity is still my captor. A click, a clang, a bang, then a sudden upward pull. A flap in a muffled wind. My pod's nosedive is arrested. A heavy sway. I'm nauseous. I spit; it falls to my chest. The pod hits a solid object and turns. No more motion. Pressure on my shoulders and hips—I'm suspended face down.

Gears grind and clack. A crunch. Mechanical sounds. The pod rolls, then lifts. My head is raised. My feet are once again below me. A display panel illuminates. A digital voice announces the air outside is breathable, temperatures are good. The planet is safe. A wave of relief passes over me. I relax, briefly.

My straps release. A door appears. I reach out; it opens. The air is fresh. Out I go. On my left arm is a display device—icons on a map showing nearby locations. I look back into the pod and take the weapon. I head toward an icon through a sparse wood. Tall trees stand here and there. I hear the whisper of a stream. My arm device tells me the water is drinkable. What is this place? Why am I here? I reach the first icon: a colleague, out of his pod.

"Captain, ready for duty, sir!" he declares.

"Follow me," I say.

We head for the next icon. *Captain? What am I the captain of?* We collect eighteen more souls; all call me Captain. We have the same weapons, the same device on our arms. One man organizes the rest, then takes me aside.

"Captain, you got knocked out when we were attacked. We just got you out."

"I don't remember much."

"Not to worry, Captain. I've got your back. Our mission is to scout this planet for habitation. Our planet is nearly dead. Follow my lead."

His words cut through the fog in my brain. My sense of readiness sharpens.

We take shelter in a nearby farmhouse. This planet seems livable so far. We can breathe. The water is drinkable. The hostile force is unknown. Perhaps there aren't many of them. I step out to get some air. I see a Craft ship traverse the sky—the same hostile ship from space.

"They found us!" I yell.

The unit rallies to a defensive position. The Craft land. Bipedal soldiers stream out. Another ship lands nearby. We're surrounded. I'm caught in the crossfire of a firefight. Pain, then blood. I feel cold, blue. I pass out.

I awake in a chamber, surrounded by soldiers. They wear protective garb and speak in a foreign language. I'm a captive. *What planet is this?* They see I'm awake and speak to me. There is script on the wall; I don't know the language. Through a tiny hole in his small head, one of the soldiers says, "Where are you from? Why have you come to Earth?"

THE CLOWN

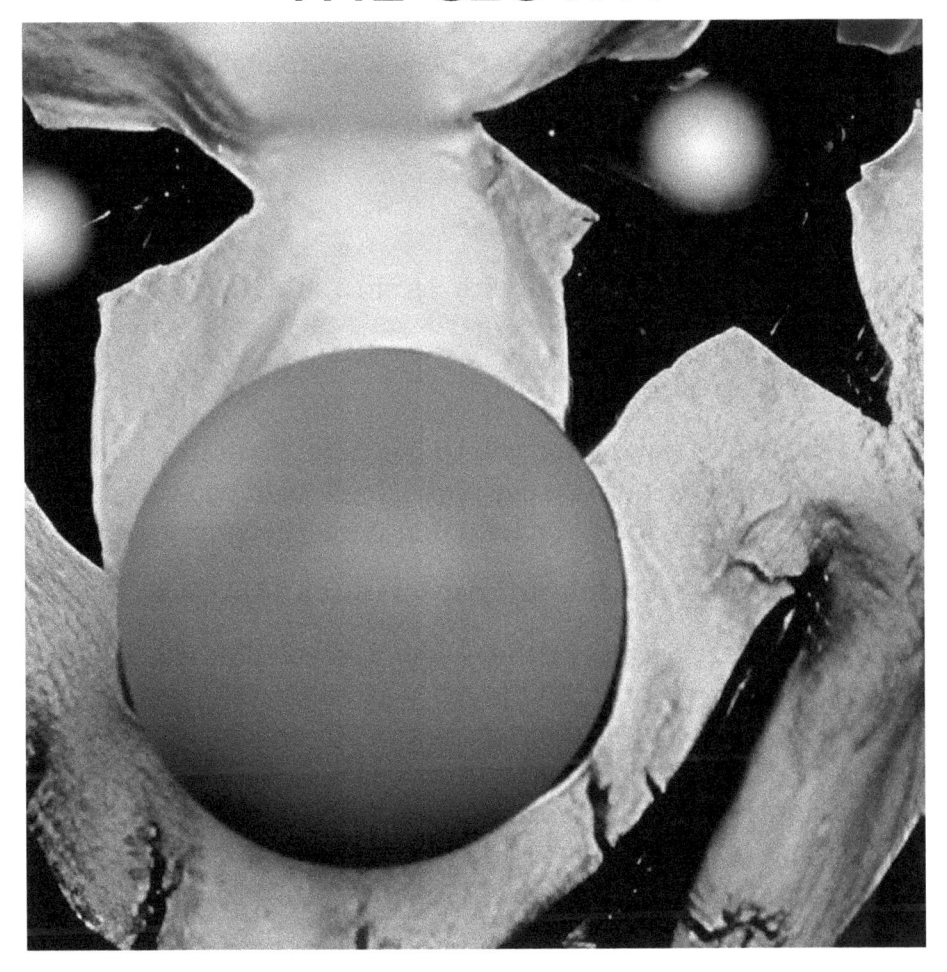

Bert lived with his sister, Julianne and her daughter, Sarah. He was between jobs. He loved his family dearly and took care of Sarah while Julianne toiled at work. Although she appreciated Bert's help with her daughter, she resented having to support him with her hard-earned money. She pressured Bert to find a job, but Bert always had excuses.

The last straw came when Julianne arranged an interview for Bert for a position she had found. Bert blew it completely.

"I got you a job. You blew off the interview. You didn't even go!" she fumed.

"I wasn't feeling well," he mumbled.

"You stayed here and played with Sarah. You didn't go. Get out!" she ordered, pointing to the door.

"You're kicking me out?"

"Yes. I'm tired of paying for you to live here. You can come back once you have a job and can pay rent. I don't want you standing in this doorway again until you have rent money in your hand!"

Bert left the house. Sarah's birthday was just a week away.

Two days before Sarah's birthday, the doorbell chimed. Julianne looked out the window. The porch was empty. She gripped the door handle, hesitated, then opened it. An envelope lay on the birchwood boards, her name written boldly across the front—like it was shouting at her. She knew it was from Bert. Inside the note read: "I have a job but no rent money. I'll be qualified to stand in your doorway soon, I assure you." Julianne broke down. She loved her brother and yearned for his success.

On Sarah's birthday, the doorbell rang again. Sarah rushed to answer it. She opened the door to find a clown balanced on his hands, his face painted white and a rubber nose perched on his beak. His red, flaccid boots dangled from where his head should have been. His tent-like coveralls hid a swirl of colorful undergarments.

"Happy Birthday!" the clown trumpeted in a screechy voice. He flopped his upside-down feet, making Sarah laugh.

"Can he come in, Mommy?" Sarah asked.

The clown remained in place, hands firmly on the porch.

"Who hired you? Was it my brother Bert?" Julianne asked warily.

"Almost, Julianne. The clown will stand in your doorway on his feet once he gets paid," Bert smiled.

THE SINK

Sam is called to an emergency at 2:00 am on a Saturday night. He drives to a house in the suburbs. All the lights are on, a party is in full swing, there are people on the front lawn and the front door stands open. Loud music blares while the grass is littered with bottles. Sam verifies the address with dispatch before he nears the house.

Sam owns his truck, the tools inside and the parts he transports. He's part if a larger plumbing company that pays him monthly to put their branding on his truck, dispatch him to calls and promote their business. Sam responds to emergencies while keeping his license valid.

"Dispatch, I'm at the emergency call. There's a party with a lot of people."

"We'll patch you through to the homeowner."

"Hello, is this the plumber?" asks Mandora, the homeowner, as music on the phone mirrors what Sam hears outside the house.

"Yes, I'm outside your home, in my truck."

"My son will come and get you."

"Okay, ma'am."

Sam stays in his truck. A young man soon presents himself and escorts Sam into the house.

"The kitchen sink has overflowed," says the young man.

"Do you know why?" asks Sam.

"We have no idea."

Sam examines the sink. The water is pearly white and white powder is scattered around the rim.

"What's this white stuff?" he asks.

"Cleaner," says Mandora.

"Did the cleaner clog the sink?"

"No, we were cleaning it and got distracted. Someone put something down the drain and clogged it. When we came back to finish cleaning, the sink was already plugged. We don't know what it is."

Worried about being there at 2:30 am with the party still active —drunk people around him and a suspicious clog—Sam calls dispatch to explain the situation. He promises he'll finish the job in twenty minutes and call back.

Standard procedure for the company requires a plumber to check in before starting a job and again after completing it. If he fails to call in after finishing, dispatch will attempt contact twice at ten-minute intervals; if there is still no response, the police are notified. A plumber's vehicle and equipment, worth over $250,000, can tempt thieves so this protocol is critical, especially at night.

Thirty minutes after his initial call, Sam's phone rings, but he doesn't answer. It rings again ten minutes later and he still fails to respond.

"We have a plumber at the following address," the plumber dispatch informs 911. "He was dispatched to repair a clogged sink and is now twenty minutes overdue on his check-in. We've run our safety protocols and lost contact with him. There's a party at the house."

"Yes, ma'am. We were at that address earlier this evening for a noise complaint. We'll dispatch a unit," replies the operator.

The police arrive at the scene. The plumbing truck sits curbside and the yard is empty except for scattered bottles. The officers draw their weapons as the open front door beckons them inside. Blaring music assaults their senses. They enter the building to find it deserted, then head to the kitchen, where three people are on the floor. The sink overflows with pearl-tinged water, bordered by a pinkish-white residue. The air smells sharp and lingers in the back of the throat. A blush of pink chalk floats in the room, like smoke with nowhere to go. The officers quickly cover their faces, check for life signs and drag the three civilians to safety.

"We need an ambulance—three civilians down," one officer radios.

Fresh air revives the woman, the young man and Sam.

After a moment, an officer asks, "What happened in there? This is the second time we've been to this address tonight."

Still dazed, the young man admits, "You left so quickly the first time. We thought you were coming in the house. We had to call a plumber. We didn't know the sink would plug when we washed the cocaine down the drain."

Author's note: The Sink

I was sitting, wondering what to write, when I glanced at the kitchen sink and had a sudden idea: write a story about an overflowing sink and a body on the floor.

SUBSIDIARY

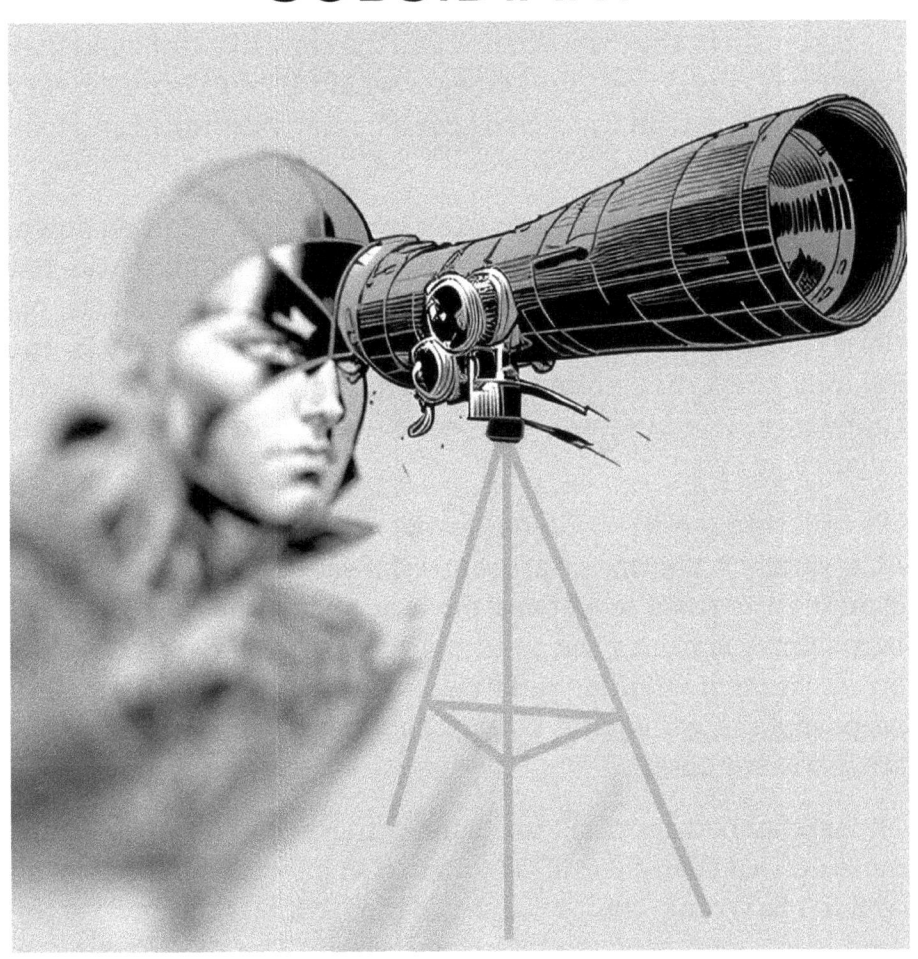

Lies were thrown about like shuttlecocks at a badminton tournament. The conference was in its second day. Vendor account representatives would say anything to make a sale. Buyers wanted free handouts and promised anything to get them. The conference coordinator lied her way to peace and goodwill among vendors and attendees. The caterer held back so everyone was treated the same—except for those who weren't. Speakers wanted the best ratings, the most airtime and the most likes for what they had to say. Everyone told whoever would listen whatever they thought that person wanted to hear. The watcher smiled and took notes as he observed the crowds.

The FBI showed up at the door. The conference was locked down. No one was sure why. The name of body in the alley was not revealed to anyone at the conference: a conference attendee, his throat slashed with a catering knife, his body dumped. In the FBI interviews, his colleagues agreed his notes could be read with confidence. His program was meticulously outlined, his notes impeccably clear.

His trail through the conference was revealed through his notes. At a vendor's booth, an account representative pushed a rifle, claiming the AMX scope was the best on the market. The dead man's notes spoke to the contrary. He attended a speech on the preservation of wildlife, wetlands and hunting—on how a quality scope makes for merciful killing. The speaker affirmed the AMX scope was the best.

The conference coordinator claimed there was no other scope more desired than the AMX. In an exchange with a hunter—who couldn't be wrong—he, too, asserted the AMX was the one. Yet the dead man's own research rebuked them all. The AMX scope was not the ultimate.

In the corner of his notebook, a small note laid bare the truth: the conference organizer was owned by AMX's parent company. Everyone at the conference had been coached to sell AMX. The dead man had uncovered a conspiracy.

He was last seen eating lunch alone; his notes had been left in a conference room, discovered by catering staff and returned to him during lunch. Sometime after, his throat was slit with a catering knife. The catering company was owned by the same parent company as AMX.

THE BUCKET

A heavy haul truck stopped across the street. The excavator was offloaded in front of an abandoned house. The operator maneuvered the machine through the yard. He positioned it to demolish the house. We watched from our thirtieth-floor apartment across the street. The bucket settled on the grass. His door opened. We expected him to check the property. We turned away to make coffee.

"Was it nine or ten homeless people we counted there last night?" I asked my wife.

She couldn't remember. A minute later, we turned back to the window. Three people ran through the side yard of the house. The excavator door was closed. The bucket was planted in the living room of the house.

The excavator door opened.

STARTER

On April 15, 1990, I was born—a simple process, really. On Day 1 a cup of filtered water joins a cup of flour—the kind with a good amount of gluten. Soon, the sound of metal tapping against glass follows: a swirling motion, devoid of queasiness. The smell of raw flour fills the air. I spend the day alone on the counter, sheltered from the sun but kept warm.

Day two. Another round of water and flour is added—though half as much today. More swirling and metallic tapping ensue as I sit on the counter, awaiting my first breath—the one only I can give. Then, three more days pass in a cycle of swirling, tapping and waiting.

At last, my breath arrives. I remain captive in my glass house. A house with no vertical barrier. I breathe, I grow, I expand upward. My breath originates from my core: I bubble with air pockets and blister above my glass house rim. Having achieved full strength, I relax. This assertion of existence is my triumph. My air pockets dissipate as bubbles burst and fade and the blisters melt away, leaving only a hint of residue. As the residue dries—rigid, stiff and flaky— it stands as evidence of my success. I am now ready for my purpose.

For years, I am consumed daily. I am a creator. My life is long and fragile. I depend on being fed with love and care. I breathe, I relax. My house is dry, stiff and flaky— a testament to my daily triumph. A hint of residue always lingers. I am ready once more. Born of flour and water. I have family.

I am now over thirty years old and have been productive. I have breathed life into more than nine thousand offspring. Every day, I bubble, I swell, flowing beyond the limits of my glass house. I ferment, releasing gas into the world. My gift is sourdough bread. I am the starter.

F. C. HOLMES

Author's note: Starter

This was the first piece of short fiction I wrote, inspired by my love of making sourdough bread. In it, the starter sits on the counter as it bubbles and churns. I embellished its age and offspring.

BOOKS IN THE SERIES

BOOK 1

Memory is a fiction we keep rewriting...

BOOK 2

We wear the stories we survive...

BOOK 3

We become the truths we bury...

BOOK 4

Some echoes never fade…